214
ways to say
I love you

214

ways to say
I love you

Julian Biddle

PINNACLE BOOKS

PINNACLE BOOKS are published by

Kensington Publishing Corp.
850 Third Avenue
New York, NY 10022

Pinnacle and the P logo Reg. U.S. Pat. & TM Off.

First Pinnacle Books Printing: February, 1996
ISBN: 0-7860-0234-4

Printed in the United States of America

The author would like to thank the following:

Grace Alicea, Tracy Bernstein, Dale Coots, Elizabeth Crowe,
Mary T. Denton, Elise Donner, Lisa Filippatos (Thea and Lily, too!),
Claire Hurd, Enza Lozito, Krista Joy Mervine, Annette Morgenroth,
Jeannie Garrison Ryburn, and Elizabeth Schoch.

This book is dedicated to the love of my life.

1. Does your love have cold feet—as in icy toes? Get some colorful, snuggly socks to keep those toes you love warm.

2. Tea for two. Or coffee for two. Or a tall, cool drink for two. But find a private time during the day for only the two of you. No children. No pets. And certainly not the television or the telephone.

3. Fido needs to be walked and Fluffy's litter needs to be changed. Okay, okay, they're not your pets and not your responsibility. But sometimes your love could use the extra help. And extra help is always appreciated. (A big hint: never remind your mate of your assistance. You're not looking for a raise. This is love.)

4. Revisit the place where you met and fell in love. The trees have grown taller; your love will have grown stronger.

5. Photographs may not do your love justice, or so they say. But if you take your favorite picture of him/her and frame it, that says so much. Place it on your nightstand or desk to show that your thoughts are on him/her all through the day.

6. Don't forget the best medicine for so many ailments is a warm hug. Those unexpected ones—in the middle of watching a Little League game or in the middle of the night—are the best! A tender hug in the morning is a memory that will last all day.

7. Plan a little getaway just for two. If an entire weekend isn't possible, at least one night together can make the difference. And *vive la différence!*

8. Roses are red,
Violets are blue,
Flowers on a Tuesday
will always do.

9. What people refer to as *pillow talk* is poorly named. It really should be called *pillow listen* for the best results.

10. Buy or rent your sweetheart's favorite flick. Whether it's *Dirty Harry* or *When Harry Met Sally . . .* , remember, it's for love.

11. Set the night to music—especially *her* favorite kind, even if it's not yours.

12. Face it, you have never been punctual. Ask your mother. Even *she* says you were born late. If it drives someone you love crazy, clean up your act.

13. Experience counts. When you give a gift for an anniversary or a birthday, it doesn't always need to be a *thing*. It can be an experience. Try theater or ballgame tickets, or a gift certificate for a massage.

14. While we're on the subject of gift-giving . . . don't wait until the very last moment to come up with the perfect idea. Listen for hints all year round and write them down.

15. It's never too late in a relationship to compliment your partner for having good looks. Sure, there may be some gray hairs, some undeniable wrinkles, but that doesn't mean your love has changed. And it doesn't mean you shouldn't say a nice word to the one you love.

16. Remind your sweetie of upcoming birthdays and anniversaries. Not yours—Sweetie's mom's birthday, for instance.

17. Offer her a jacket when it's too cold. See to it that he stays warm once he's done that.

18. Necking tip: the back of the neck is a very sensitive spot on most human beings. Be sure your honey has enough neck rubs so that both of you can enjoy the other kind pain-free.

19. A little farther south on the human body is that large expanse—
the back. Back rubs are a bit more complicated and deserve
your full, undivided attention for a good half hour. Use oils or
ointments for the most soothing results.

20. Two people who share a home, a life, and each other's love should also share in the decision-making process when it comes to decorating that home. No one should live with furniture he can't stand. No one should live with colors that grate. Always consult with one another when choosing important items for the home.

21. Throw a surprise party for someone you love.

22. Your love has always wanted a fluffy little puppy. Tomorrow is a good time for you to bring one home. Things will definitely develop—from puppy love to deep, everlasting devotion. And the puppy will be fun, too!

23. If your sweetheart has been hinting that your current hairdo is a no-no, snip those locks the way he/she likes them.

24. The room is filled with noisy people and you both wonder why you came. Sweetie is trapped in a dull conversation with a relative's relative's relative. Give "the look," that special smile-and-wink that you always use only with each other.

25. Love is sometimes a matter of degree. He's too hot. She's too cold. Compromise on the perfect temperature for the both of you.

26. Don't forget to leave a light on.

27. When you rough it by going camping, try a sleeping bag for two.

28. Always say "thank you" with a kiss for a job done for you by someone you love.

29. Plan a sleighride for two and share a blanket.

30. Be the first one to wake up and make the morning coffee.

31. Develop a wicked backhand while playing a love match together.

32. The words "I've missed you" are always important to say and nice to hear.

33. Be the first to kiss your loved one goodnight.

34. Be the first to kiss your loved one good morning.

35. Give your children lots of hugs.

36. Give your children lots of kisses.

37. Give your children lots of space to be themselves.

38. Give your parents a telephone call more than once a week.

39. It may begin with only a single spark, but a cozy fire in the fireplace can warm more than just a chill—it'll warm your hearts.

40. Bogart and Bergman drank champagne the day Paris fell. She wore blue, he wore a smile. Champagne cannot guarantee anything so dramatic, but a bottle can add sparkle to a mundane Monday.

41. Buy two instant lottery tickets—one for each of you. (Share the winnings.)

42. Your children belong to both of you. Spend time with them so that your loved one can spend some time alone.

43. Just because you're now a parent doesn't mean you've stopped being someone's child. Invite your parents—and your mate's—to share in the joy of your new baby.

44. Bite your tongue. Allow your loved one to have the floor when voicing an opinion that happens not to be yours.

45. Express yourself. Make your position clear about important matters. But don't have a big fight with someone you love in front of other people.

46–47. Go ahead, let him win once in a while. Turnabout is fair play, so let her win sometime, too. We're talking games here—board games, card games—not the ones people play to spite each other.

48. Cultivate friends together.

49. Cultivate your garden together.

50. Entertain new friends together.

51. Entertain new ideas together.

52. Understand that not all husbands have the all-knowing powers of Ward Cleaver.

53. Understand that not all wives wear dresses and pearls all day like Donna Reed.

54. Understand that children never behave like the ones on television.

55. Do not get frustrated by this knowledge.

56. Buy ice cream cones for two.

57. Take a hike. Or a walk. Or a stroll down a quiet country lane. Or a city sidewalk. Hold hands. Walk arm-in-arm. Share your thoughts on the tall trees, or the tall buildings.

58. Share your dreams for the future.

59. Share your dreams of the night before.

60. Play Mickey and Minnie Mouse by making your personal computer fun for both of you.

61. Keep the treat in Halloween. Dress up as famous duos: Raggedy Ann and Andy; Boris and Natasha; Archie and Edith.

62. Keep the "thanks" in Thanksgiving.

63. Keep good cheer in New Year's.

64. Follow your love wherever life takes you.

65. Lead the way. Gently.

66. Tickling is not always fun for the tickled. But one little tickle can't hurt.

67. When the doctor orders plenty of bedrest for your sweetheart, be sure you're there to administer tender loving care.

68. Say "please" whenever you have a request.

69. Offer plenty of "thank yous" when the task is completed.

70. Find time to give a good foot massage.

71. The family vacation should not be a scavenger hunt. Plan your route, call ahead for rooms for the night, find out what restaurants are nearby.

72. Offer to drive the car after your honey has spent several hours behind the wheel.

73. Fix her a hot chocolate on a cold, wintry afternoon.

74. Give him the part of the Sunday newspaper that you both can't wait to read.

75. Build your garden with the rocks the two of you collect from the different states you visit.

76. When you're picking up some magazines for yourself, don't forget to include one of his favorites.

77. Designate "special" cups for each other's use when drinking coffee or tea. (Don't be afraid to update these pieces every few years.)

78. Pitch in when it comes time to cut the grass. At the very least, prepare some lemonade.

79. Pitch in when it comes time to rake the leaves. At the very least, prepare a cup of coffee.

80. Pitch in when it comes time to shovel the snow. At the very least, prepare a cup of hot chocolate.

81. Use one wall in your home as a gallery for all your framed photographs. Don't limit it to just the two of you—hang pictures of the entire family, all friends, and your distant relatives.

82. Volunteer to do good works together. It could be at the local fire department or the senior citizen home nearby or the hospital in the community.

83. Dinnertime is the most important part of the day for a family that loves each other. Be sure everybody eats together.

84. If you weren't the one to prepare the meal, you should be the one to clean up.

85. Always call home when you're away on a business trip.

86. Always bring back a gift from the city where you stayed.

87. Always send Mom and Dad a postcard when you're away.

88. In the wintertime, turn down the thermostat so that the two of you can snuggle. Make your own kind of heat.

89. Have a snowball fight. But make sure you don't aim to hurt.

90. Buy her fine lingerie—just for the fun of it.

91. Pamper him—buy him the expensive tools he wants.

92. Butter each other's toast. Notice how the heat makes it melt.

93. Don't *help* with the housework. *Do* the housework!

94. Write her a poem and don't worry if it sounds silly.

95. Give someone a Teddy bear.

96. Both of you call in "sick." Stay in bed until you both get "better." It may be just what the doctor ordered.

97–113. Carefully plan out a candlelight dinner for two. Serve it at midnight. Choose a good wine and the foods the both of you normally can't afford. Light the entire room with candles. While you're eating, pretend you're in some cozy French restaurant on the Champs Élysée. While in Paris, catch the sights . . . of each other's smiles. Play footsie under the table. Feed each other off your plates. Whisper in each other's ears—in English or French or whatever secret language the two of you share—about how much you're enjoying coming to this private hideaway. Snack on each other's earlobes since you're in the vicinity. Blow out all the

candles but one to gain suitably intimate lighting. Gaze into each other's eyes. Caress the smiling face you see through the flickering candlelight. Nuzzle closely. Feel that special warmth. It's love.

114. Clean up in the morning.

115. Your honey has been coveting something a little too pricy. Start a special savings account to fulfill your loved one's wish.

116. Turn the dial on the radio *back* to someone's favorite station after you've listened to yours.

117. Buy a date book. Circle a date. Keep it special just for the two of you.

118. Engage Uncle Mike in conversation, even though he's not your uncle. And keep up the small talk just to please your loved one.

119. Handle each other with kid gloves. Buy matching pairs.

120. Spend a little time together in a hot tub. See what kind of steam you make.

121. Pretend your pick-up is a Rolls Royce. Just for the night.

122. Pretend your Rolls Royce is a pick-up. Just for the night.

123. Earlobes are meant to be nibbled. Do it often.

124. Don't forget to buy earmuffs to protect those objects of your affection.

125. *Melrose Place* is even better when you watch it together.

126. Make, buy, or otherwise acquire your loved one's favorite desserts whenever possible.

127. Don't knock the joys of *As the World Turns*.

128. Patch a torn pair of pants.

129. Patch up an argument.

130. If you can find one, go to a drive-in movie. Mom and Dad in the front seat, the kids nodding off in the back. And after the tots are asleep, Mom and Dad can smooch and nuzzle. Just like in the movies.

131. One of the very best ways to show you care is to stay healthy. Your loved ones want to have you around for a long, long time.

132. Hold each other's feet when the other is doing sit-ups.

133. Towel each other off.

134. Eat plenty of vegetables together.

135. Introduce your children to art. Not Art from down the street, but the kind that hangs in museums.

136. Introduce your children to music, and not just your own personal favorites, but all kinds.

137. Go ice skating together. Hold each other up.

138. Don't be competitive. It's easier than it sounds, but remember that Monopoly is not a blood sport.

139. Don't be shy. Especially when you meet your loved one's friends and relatives.

140. Help your honey avoid unnecessary sweets.

141. Everybody needs a little sweetening every now and then. Put the sugar in your sweet's coffee. Go ahead, stir it up.

142. Be a hero to a neighborhood youngster who needs help.

143. Remember your loved ones in your prayers.

144. Remember to pray.

145. Remember the song *Button up your overcoat*. Do it for your loved one. And top it off with a scarf and a hug around the neck.

146. Going strapless only works for evening gowns. Wear a seat-belt. And tell everybody else to wear one, too.

147. Live an interesting life together, but don't even think about going on a talk show.

148. If you can't find the "perfect" card, devise one of your own.

149. Remember to mail the card in time to arrive for the special day.

150. Keep up family traditions.

151. Keep faith.

152. At holiday time, think up a theme for your honey's gifts.

153. If you give a pepper mill, don't forget the peppercorns.

150. Keep up family traditions.

151. Keep faith.

152. At holiday time, think up a theme for your honey's gifts.

153. If you give a pepper mill, don't forget the peppercorns.

154. Generally speaking, a tie is a nice gift for someone you hardly know, not for someone you share your life with.

155. Generally speaking, cash is not a thoughtful gift for your life partner.

156. If your loved one is allergic to pine, don't insist on having a real Christmas tree.

157. Encourage those you love to give up the smoking habit. You'll all breathe easier.

158. Surprise a busy (or lonely) someone with a home cooked meal delivered right to their door. For that special case, of course, there's always breakfast in bed.

159. Squeeze fresh oranges for each other.

160. If someone you love is going on a long business trip or your kids are headed off to summer camp, write them a letter before they leave so they'll have mail waiting for them.

161. Don't forget to tuck your children in every night.

162. Homemade apple pies are the best. Learn to make them from scratch.

163. Don't put the basketball hoop too high for your son (or daughter) to play.

164. Be sure the kids have chores to do so that they learn what the word responsibility means.

165. Give the kids a break from responsibility.

166. Pay compliments to your children for a job well done.

167. Pay attention when your children need help.

168. One of the greatest things a parent can do is to teach the children to love each other. Nothing lasts quite as long as the affection between siblings.

169. Send your brother or sister a note just to say hi.

170. While you're at it, why not put together a photo album of you and your siblings from the "good old days" and send it along?

171. Invite your sister-in-law or brother-in-law into your circle of friends.

172. It doesn't need to be expensive, and it certainly doesn't have to come from Tiffany's, but buy your love a small piece of jewelry every now and then.

173. Do something *wild* together. Who cares about looking foolish at least once in your life?

174. Explore new terrain. Don't be afraid to discover each other's body parts.

175. Keep the funny stories and jokes coming. The best times are those when everybody is laughing—but never at someone's expense.

176. Find a place where the two of you can receive back rubs at the same time.

177. Teach your wife to shave you.

178. Remember the birthdays of your nieces and nephews.

179. Grandma should always be asked to hold the baby. She's held plenty of babies, probably even you.

180. Ask Granddad lots of questions. He most likely knows the answers. He's been around a while. Knows his stuff.

181. Make plans for your retirement—not only financial ones but dreamy plans, too. Will you learn Italian, nestle in a cabin, sail the seas? Talking about your future together is very romantic.

182–185. When your loved one has had a bad day, follow this recipe: tell a joke. Put on a smile. Divert attention to pleasant things, such as your loving kisses. Otherwise lighten the mood with plenty of hugs.

186. Maybe his invention is a little wacky, but don't discourage the unknown. Don't you wonder what Mrs. Edison thought about that lightbulb idea?

187. If she wants to visit the stars' homes in Hollywood, indulge her fantasy.

188. Build the kids a treehouse.

189. Let the kids win at checkers.

190. Teach the kids how to program the VCR so that they can tape *Barney*.

191. Just because you're married doesn't mean you can't still go dancing.

192. Teach him new steps.

193. Put together a family tree. This is a great excuse to contact faraway relatives "just to catch up."

194. Demonstrate to your children that you want to be part of their lives . . . a good way is to refer to your children's friends by their rightfully given names.

195. Wash her car.

196. Wash his dog.

197. Wash each other.

198. Solve the mysteries of life together like you're Nick and Nora Charles.

199. Take the whole family to the ice hockey game. Even Aunt Estelle.

200. Take the whole family to the dance recital. Don't forget Grandma and Granddad.

201. Remind your child to bundle up against the cold. Ignore this once your child has reached adulthood.

202. Brush her hair.

203. Help with the crossword puzzles only when asked.

204. Be a den mother or a scout leader or a baseball coach. But curb your expectations and show no favoritism to your own.

205. Never act like Erica Kane.

206. Try to be as witty as Seinfeld.

207. Bake her birthday cake.

208. Wipe the ice from her windshield.

209. Wipe his brow.

210. Kiss in the moonlight.

211. Kiss in the dark.

212. Kiss often.

213. Choose a pet name and stick with it, especially during intimate moments. Don't be *pet-rified* to use, Darling, Sweetheart, or the ever-lovable Honey Bunny.

214. Write a book and dedicate it to the love of your life.